CALGARY PUBLIC LIBRARY

JUL   2015

Library and Archives Canada Cataloguing in Publication

Cole, Kathryn, author
Reptile flu : a story about communication /
by Kathryn Cole ; illustrated by Qin Leng.

(I'm a great little kid series)
Co-published by: Boost Child Abuse Prevention & Intervention.
ISBN 978-1-927583-61-6 (bound)

1. Communication—Juvenile fiction. I. Leng, Qin, illustrator
II. Boost Child Abuse Prevention & Intervention, publisher III. Title.

PS8605.O4353R46 2015   jC813'.6   C2014-908042-5

Copyright © 2015 Boost Child Abuse Prevention & Intervention and Kathryn Cole
Illustrations by Qin Leng
Design by Melissa Kaita
Printed and bound in China

*Boost Child Abuse Prevention & Intervention gratefully acknowledges the generous support
of Rogers Communications for funding the development and publication of the Prevention
Program Series. Rogers Communications is an important partner in our efforts to prevent
abuse and violence in children's lives.*

*Second Story Press gratefully acknowledges the support of the Ontario Arts Council and the
Canada Council for the Arts for our publishing program. We acknowledge the financial support
of the Government of Canada through the Canada Book Fund.*

Published by
Second Story Press
20 Maud Street, Suite 401
Toronto, Ontario, Canada
M5V 2M5
www.secondstorypress.ca

Reptile Flu
A story about communication

written by Kathryn Cole
illustrated by Qin Leng

Second Story Press

Ms. Crosby passed out the worksheets. "Now that you know all about reptiles," she said, "I have a surprise. Let's get this work done first, and then I'll tell you about it."

The kids settled down to work and soon everyone was drawing pictures of their favorite reptiles.

Everyone except Kamal. He didn't have a favorite. The very thought of reptiles sent shivers down his spine. He decided to draw the one he was least afraid of – a little green gecko. He made it extra small on his paper.

Kamal peeked to his left. Devon hummed as he drew a Komodo dragon with a long, slithery tongue. "That's scary," Kamal mumbled. But Devon was busy drawing and humming and didn't answer.

Kamal peeked to his right. Claire's favorite reptile was a huge snapping turtle with a nasty-looking beak. "*Ugh!*" Kamal shuddered, but Claire wasn't looking at him, so she didn't notice.

"Mine's a giant boa constrictor, see?" Dee-Dee shoved her drawing close to Kamal's face.

"That's horrible!" said Kamal, pushing the paper away.

"Well your puny gecko isn't much to look at either," Dee-Dee huffed. "How rude!"

They're only drawings, Kamal told himself. *The real reptiles live far, far away.*

Then something awful happened. With a big smile, Ms. Crosby handed out permission forms for a class trip. "There's a special reptile show on at the museum, and we're all going!" she said. "Have your form signed at home and return it to me. And don't lose it. You won't want to miss this."

"Are they *live* reptiles?" asked Lin.

"Can we hold them?" Joseph wanted to know.

"Is there a boa constrictor?" That was Dee-Dee.

"Yes, yes, and yes!" answered Ms. Crosby. Everybody cheered.

Everybody except Kamal. "*I* want to miss it," he said. But the cheering drowned out his words. He would have to try again.

Kamal stayed behind after school. "Do you have something to say, Kamal?" asked Ms. Crosby.

"No…well, yes…sort of." The room was quiet, Ms. Crosby was looking right at him, and she wasn't doing anything else. This was Kamal's chance to tell her he was afraid of reptiles. He took a deep breath…. He opened his mouth…. "I like your dress," he said.

"Thank you, Kamal. Is that all?"

"I also like rabbits…a lot."

"Rabbits are nice," said Ms. Crosby.

"Not like reptiles," offered Kamal. There. He'd said it.

"No, not like reptiles. You wouldn't be a bit nervous about reptiles, would you, Kamal?"

The way she asked made Kamal think he shouldn't admit he was terrified. What if Ms. Crosby laughed? What if she told the others? What if they teased him the way he had teased Shaun about riding his bike?

"Me?" he said. "Of course not. I could wrestle an alligator if I had to."

Ms. Crosby chuckled. "Well you won't have to do that – not next week, anyway. Have a good night, Kamal."

Then he remembered the permission form. If it wasn't signed, he couldn't go to the museum! He would have to lose it somehow. But before he could do anything, his mom opened his schoolbag to put his lunch inside.

"What's this?" she asked. "Another school trip? Hmm. This one costs seven dollars." She reached for her purse.

"That's too much, Mom. You have better things to do with that money, right? Don't sign it," said Kamal. "I'll just stay home with Gramps."

"And miss the trip? I should say not. It's very sweet of you, darling, but these are memories you will always have. They are precious." Kamal's mom signed the form, wrote the check, and tucked them in his bag.

I'll remember this all right, Kamal thought.

Kamal tried again. His dad was vacuuming the living room.

"Dad? We're going on a trip to the museum next week to see creepy, disgusting, scaly reptiles, and I—"

"That's great, son," Kamal's father said without looking up from his work. "All kids your age love that sort of thing. Tell me about it when you get back."

Kamal sighed. Maybe his sister would listen.

Kamal found her in her room with headphones on, listening to music. He waved and called her name. "I'm afraid of reptiles," he muttered.

She didn't even notice. *Hopeless*, Kamal thought. *She might as well be in outer space.*

At school Kamal handed in his form. He gave up trying to tell anyone how afraid he was. No one was listening. Besides, there were five more days until the museum trip. Maybe by then he could develop a bad case of "reptile flu."

On the day of the class trip, everyone was excited. The school bus waited outside while they put on coats and boots.

By now, Kamal was so upset he couldn't even zip up his jacket. He had *not* come down with the flu that morning. He had told everybody about his problem, but they just didn't get it.

Kamal started to feel kind of angry. His dad was wrong. Not *all* kids his age liked creepy, crawly things. His mom was wrong.

This would *not* be a precious memory. Even Ms. Crosby was wrong. He'd been wrestling alligators in his sleep all week. Didn't anyone care how *he* felt? Weren't *his* feelings important? Now it was too late.
   Or was it?

Kamal dropped his boots with a loud thud. A few heads turned.

Kamal stood up straight and tall. A few more kids stopped talking.

Kamal took a big, deep breath. He tried again. Looking directly at his classmates, Kamal spoke loudly and clearly. "Listen to me! I have something important to say. I am terrified of reptiles. I don't want to touch them or hold them or be anywhere near them. And I *really*, REALLY, *REALLY* don't want to go to the reptile show!"

Everything stopped.

No one moved.

No one spoke.

No one laughed.

Ms. Crosby broke the silence. "Kamal, is that what you tried to tell me last week?"

Now Kamal *was* feeling slightly flu-ish. He nodded his head.

"Well, you've certainly said it now. Good for you. It took courage to speak up in front of everybody. If I promise to be your partner and stay right beside you at the museum, will you come with us?"

All eyes were on Kamal. "Maybe…." he said, standing a little taller. "I guess so."

"That's a relief," said Ms. Crosby. "Because I could use a brave person beside me when we get to the geckos. I'm terrified of them."

"You *are*?" Kamal was amazed. "You should have told me before! Don't worry, I'll be your partner. We'll do this together."

On the bus Devon raised his hand. "Ms. Crosby? I'm brave too. I'm afraid of sharks."

"I'm afraid of heights," added Claire.

"Spiders!" Nadia called out.

"Big purple rats with red spots!" Shaun shouted.

"What a brave bunch you are," commented Ms. Crosby. Soon they were all being silly and laughing.

All but Dee-Dee. "Now hear this," she announced in her big booming voice. I'm not afraid of anything! And that's the truth."

No one doubted it.

At the end of the day, the museum guide asked who wanted to hold a newly hatched alligator. Kamal raised his hand and spoke right up. "I do! I used to be afraid of alligators, but now I'm brave." The cute baby reptile tickled his hand.

Now this, is a precious memory, he thought.

For Grown-ups

About Communication

Communication is the process of sending and receiving verbal and non-verbal messages. It involves understanding feelings and recognizing that everyone has the right to express feelings without infringing on the rights of others. Children increase their skills and confidence as communicators when they receive the support they need to talk about what is important to them.

Parents can support their children to develop communication skills:

- **Talk with them:** Give lots of opportunity for children to participate in conversations.

- **Listen to them:** Recognize that what children have to say is important.

- **Respect them:** When you consider your children's feelings they learn that everyone's feelings are valued.

- **Create the environment:** Surround your children with positive communication where ideas and feelings are expressed openly.

- **Guide them:** Recognize that words are powerful; choose each word with care. Children are always listening, even when you are not speaking to them directly.

- **Set a good example:** Children notice inconsistencies in our verbal and non-verbal communication. Make sure your words match what your expressions and body language are saying.